HOPSCOTCH TWISTY TALES

The Pied Piper
and the
Wrong Song

by Laura North and Scoular Anderson

W

This story is based on the traditional fairy tale,
The Pied Piper of Hamelin but with a new twist.
You can read the original story in
Hopscotch Fairy Tales. Can you make
up your own twist for the story?

First published in 2013 by
Franklin Watts
338 Euston Road
London
NW1 3BH

Franklin Watts Australia
Level 17/207 Kent Street
Sydney
NSW 2000

Text © Laura North 2013
Illustrations © Scoular Anderson 2013

The rights of Laura North to be identified as the author
and Scoular Anderson as the illustrator of this Work have been asserted
in accordance with the Copyright, Designs and Patents Act, 1988.

A CIP catalogue record for this book is available
from the British Library.

ISBN 978 1 4451 1632 7 (hbk)
ISBN 978 1 4451 1638 9 (pbk)

Series Editor: Melanie Palmer
Series Advisor: Catherine Glavina
Series Designer: Peter Scoulding

Printed in China

Franklin Watts is a division of
Hachette Children's Books,
an Hachette UK company
www.hachette.co.uk

To Dylan — L.N.

In the town of Hamelin
there were rats everywhere.

"The Pied Piper can help us,"
said the Mayor.
"He plays a magic pipe that
makes the rats go away."

So the Pied Piper arrived in town.
"I will get rid of your rats!"
he promised.

Rid-a-Rat

"If you can do that," said the Mayor, "I will give you ten bags of gold."

"No problem," said the Pied Piper.
He took out his magic pipe and
started to play.

The rats looked up at the Pied
Piper. Not one of them moved.

But one by one, all the cows in the town started to follow the Pied Piper's magic song.

"Oh no!" said the Mayor.

"What are you doing?"

"I don't know what went wrong!"
said the Pied Piper. "Let me
try again."

This time all the pigs began to follow the Pied Piper, and danced in a line to his tune.

"Come back!" the Mayor shouted
after the pigs. "There goes all
our bacon!"

"Oh dear," said the Pied Piper.

"This doesn't usually happen."

"Let me try again," said the Pied
Piper. He started to play.

All the farmers started to dance
along merrily, heading for the hills.

The farmers left their gates open and their farm animals escaped!

The goats were eating the flowers.

The pigs were sitting in armchairs.

And the cows got into bed.

One clever boy called Peter had an idea. "Take these," he said, and gave everyone earmuffs.

"You won't be able to hear anything that the Pied Piper plays."

The Pied Piper said,

"I know I've got it right this time!"

He played his magic pipe. But

nobody moved at all.

No one heard a thing.

Not one rat, cow, pig or farmer.

And the rats were still everywhere!
The Mayor gave up. The townspeople
paid the Pied Piper to go away
instead!

Put these pictures in the correct order.
Which event do you think is most important?
Now try writing the story in your own words!

Puzzle 2

Choose the correct speech bubbles for each character. Can you think of any others? Turn over to find the answers.

Answers

Puzzle 1

The correct order is: 1c, 2e, 3f, 4b, 5a, 6d

Puzzle 2

The Pied Piper: 1, 3, 6

The Mayor: 2, 4, 5

Look out for more Hopscotch Twisty Tales and Fairy Tales:

TWISTY TALES

The Lovely Duckling
ISBN 978 1 4451 1627 3*
ISBN 978 1 4451 1633 4
Hansel and Gretel and the Green Witch
ISBN 978 1 4451 1628 0*
ISBN 978 1 4451 1634 1
The Emperor's New Kit
ISBN 978 1 4451 1629 7*
ISBN 978 1 4451 1635 8
Rapunzel and the Prince of Pop
ISBN 978 1 4451 1630 3*
ISBN 978 1 4451 1636 5
Dick Whittington Gets on his Bike
ISBN 978 1 4451 1631 0*
ISBN 978 1 4451 1637 2
The Pied Piper and the Wrong Song
ISBN 978 1 4451 1632 7*
ISBN 978 1 4451 1638 9
The Princess and the Frozen Peas
ISBN 978 1 4451 0675 5
Snow White Sees the Light
ISBN 978 1 4451 0676 2

The Elves and the Trendy Shoes
ISBN 978 1 4451 0678 6
The Three Frilly Goats Fluff
ISBN 978 1 4451 0677 9
Princess Frog
ISBN 978 1 4451 0679 3
Rumpled Stilton Skin
ISBN 978 1 4451 0680 9
Jack and the Bean Pie
ISBN 978 1 4451 0182 8
Brownilocks and the Three Bowls of Cornflakes
ISBN 978 1 4451 0183 5
Cinderella's Big Foot
ISBN 978 1 4451 0184 2
Little Bad Riding Hood
ISBN 978 1 4451 0185 9
Sleeping Beauty – 100 Years Later
ISBN 978 1 4451 0186 6

FAIRY TALES
The Three Little Pigs
ISBN 978 0 7496 7905 7
Little Red Riding Hood
ISBN 978 0 7496 7907 1
Goldilocks and the Three Bears
ISBN 978 0 7496 7903 3
Hansel and Gretel
ISBN 978 0 7496 7904 0

Rapunzel
ISBN 978 0 7496 7906 4
Rumpelstiltskin
ISBN 978 0 7496 7908 8
The Elves and the Shoemaker
ISBN 978 0 7496 8543 0
The Ugly Duckling
ISBN 978 0 7496 8544 7
Sleeping Beauty
ISBN 978 0 7496 8545 4
The Frog Prince
ISBN 978 0 7496 8546 1
The Princess and the Pea
ISBN 978 0 7496 8547 8
Dick Whittington
ISBN 978 0 7496 8548 5
Cinderella
ISBN 978 0 7496 7417 5
Snow White
ISBN 978 0 7496 7418 2
The Pied Piper of Hamelin
ISBN 978 0 7496 7419 9
Jack and the Beanstalk
ISBN 978 0 7496 7422 9
The Three Billy Goats Gruff
ISBN 978 0 7496 7420 5
The Emperor's New Clothes
ISBN 978 0 7496 7421 2

*hardback